Mystery Inc. Gang Member Profile

Name:

Age:

Address:

Height:

Weight:

Likes:

Photo

Dislikes:

SCOOBY-DOO!

Map in the Mystery Machine

By Gail Herman

Illustrated by Duendes del Sur

ADVANCE PUBLISHERS

SCOOBY-DOO!

Find These Fun Activities Inside!

Check the inside back cover for fun things to do!

Bonus story-related activity strips throughout the 15 volumes.

Create your own mystery book, *Scooby-Doo The Swamp Witch!*
Color, collect, and staple the coloring pages at the end of the first 12 books in the Scooby-Doo Read & Solve mystery series.

www.advancepublishers.com
Produced by Judy O Productions, Inc.
Designed by SunDried Penguin Design
All rights reserved.
Printed in China

Scooby-Doo and his friends left Vinny's Pizza.
Velma, Fred, and Daphne waved good-bye to
Vinny and his nephew, Joe.

3

COUNTING MYSTERY

How many whole pizzas can you find in this book?

Beep!
A delivery truck whizzed by.
Scooby dove under the Mystery Machine.

4

Answer: 5

"Rook!" he cried.

"It's a map!" Velma said.

The map was old and torn.

"It looks like a mystery," Fred said.

"It looks like an old pirate's map!" Velma said.
"Maybe the map will lead to a buried treasure!"
said Daphne.

6

"Like, maybe we should not mess with a pirate's ghost," Shaggy said.

"Come on, gang!" Fred said. "We should check this out."

Fred followed the map.

He drove the van down a dirt road.

Screech!

Fred braked.

An old man stood in the way.

"Do not enter here!" the man shouted.
"This road is haunted! Turn back!"
"Good idea!" said Shaggy. "Let's go."
"Reah!" barked Scooby.
"Not so fast," Fred said.

SEEK & FIND

Find the map on this page, and then find four more on the following pages.

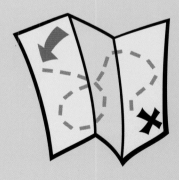

Daphne and Fred and Velma wanted to explore. "Let's split up," said Fred.

10

Shaggy and Scooby looked at each other.
To the left, the road was not so dark.
"Scooby and I will go left," Shaggy said.

11

Shaggy and Scooby took two steps.
"I think that's far enough," Shaggy
said. Then he cried, "Zoinks!"

12

Right in front of them stood a ghost.

"Ahhh!" shouted Shaggy.

"Rahhh!" shouted Scooby.

They raced down the road.
And there, up ahead, was a building.
A safe place!
Shaggy and Scooby dashed inside.

Scooby sniffed and grinned.
Shaggy's stomach rumbled.
It was a pizza kitchen!

15

"Rizza!" said Scooby.

What luck!

Scooby and Shaggy went to work —
rolling, tossing, slicing, dicing.

Pizza with everything on top —
and everything all over!

Scooby threw the dough.

Up, down. Up, down, and . . .

Find the differences between Fred on the opposite page and the one below.

Answer: his tie is purple, map is green

"Roops!" said Scooby. "Rorry!"

The dough landed on Velma's head!

"What are you guys doing here?" asked Shaggy.

"We followed the map," Daphne told him.

"It *is* a treasure map," Fred said.

"It is an ad for the Pizza Treasure Restaurant," Velma said.

19

"That's one mystery solved!" said Shaggy.
"But what about the other one?"
    "The other one?" said Velma.
    "The rhost!" Scooby cried.
    "We saw it near the van,"
Shaggy explained.

"Hmmm," Velma said. "A ghost."
She took out a napkin.
"I found this on the road — right
by the Mystery Machine. I have a
hunch about this ghost."
"Time to set a trap!"
said Fred.

Everyone turned to Scooby and Shaggy.

Scooby gulped.

"You want *us* to be the trap?" asked Shaggy.

Velma nodded.

"Ro way!" said Scooby.

"Not even for a Scooby Snack?" Daphne asked.

Scooby shook his head.

"What about two Scooby Snacks?" Velma asked.

"Rokay!" Scooby-Doo said.

Scooby and Shaggy walked down the spooky road.

"Scooby treats are just the beginning!" Shaggy told Scooby. "Soon we'll be eating pizza at Pizza Treasure!"

"Wooh!"

Zoinks! It was the ghost!

Scooby jumped into Shaggy's arms.
"Like, let's get out of here!" said Shaggy.
In a flash, they raced away.
But the ghost was right behind them!

MYSTERY MIX-UP?

Unscramble the letters
to solve these
word mysteries.

nyinv

ersraute

ikcetnh

eautnasrtr

ipnkna

All at once, Shaggy tripped.

Bump! Scooby fell right on the ghost!

"Scooby-Dooby Doo!" Scooby barked.

Velma, Fred, and Daphne ran over to see what happened.

"The costume party is over, ghost," said Velma.

Fred tore off the mask.

It was Joe, Vinny's nephew from Vinny's Pizza!

"He's scaring people from this road," Fred explained.
"Just like that old man said."

"He does not want anyone to go to Pizza Treasure," Daphne said.

"The napkin gave me the first clue," Velma added.

Shaggy looked at Joe, surprised.

"But, like, the pizza at Vinny's is great. We will never stop going there!"

"Really?" said Joe.

"Reah!" said Scooby.

"It is good to have two pizza places in town," Fred said.

"Like, then we can have a double order at two places," Shaggy said. He rubbed his rumbling stomach.

"Reah!" Scooby agreed. The gang followed Joe to Vinny's Pizza for an extra special pizza party.

Create your own bonus book!

Step 1:
Color both sides of this storybook page.

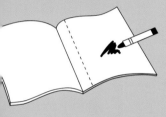

Step 2:
With an adult's supervision, carefully cut along the dotted line.

Step 3:
Repeat steps 1 and 2 in the first 12 books of the Scooby-Doo Read & Solve mystery series.

Please turn page over for further instructions.

SCOOBY-DOO!
The Swamp Witch

Adapted by Slade Stone

ADVANCE PUBLISHERS
www.advancepublishers.com
Produced by Judy O Productions, Inc.
Designed by SunDried Penguin Design
All rights reserved.

1

"What kind of creepy shortcut are you taking, Freddy?" asked Velma.

"Well, I didn't know it ran through such a spooky swamp!" said Fred.

2

Step 4:
Put all 12 cut-out pages neatly in order.

Step 5:
Staple three times on the left side of the paper stack to create the book's spine.

Step 6:
Congratulations, you have solved the mystery!

You have now created your very own Scooby-Doo storybook!

Match Scooby-Doo to his correct shadow.

1.

2.

3.

4.

The Mystery Inc. Gang

SCOOBY-DOO

The lovable, chicken-hearted Great Dane
who quivers at the sight of his own shadow and
prefers food to a mystery any day!
Favorite food: Scooby Snacks, pizza, and ice cream.

SHAGGY

Scooby-Doo's best friend, and like
Scooby, he will do anything
for a Scooby Snack.
He likes to say "zoinks," "groovy,"
and "outta sight!"